# SIMPLY BLOW A
# KISS

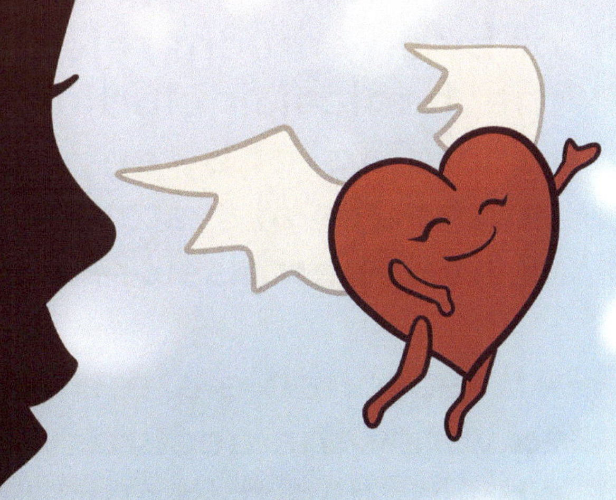

## E.L. Scholl

# DEDICATION

For my daughters, Emily and Rylee, whose adieus were the inspiration for this story.  And for my husband, Derek, whose support helped bring this story to the written page.

Have you ever had to
say goodbye to
someone you hold dear,

someone so special to
you that you always
want them near?

then I have a tip to share with you that you will want to know

SCHOOL

when all you want to do
is hold on tight and not
let go.

On days when it is hard
to watch them leave
without a tear

NOW LEAVING
TINY TOTS
LEARNING CENTER
DRIVE SAFELY

and bubbling up inside
you is a growing dread
and fear.

DBS 18

When all you want to do
is hug that person that
you miss...

the answer I have for you
is to simply blow a kiss.

A kiss that's blown is
special and you may not
be aware,
but no matter where you
send it it will always
make it there.

Though rain and snow and wind and sleet can stop it in its tracks... That kiss has made a promise, and it will always keep its pact.

You see, a kiss that's blown for one you love has a very special task. It's on a mission to spread some love and that is a tall ask.

CURRENT
LOCATION
BIOLOGY
ROOM
122
MISSION
FILE
TARGET
EDWARD
SOUTH
HIGH
SCHOOL
7

It must push through all
life's crazy things and
continue to its goal
of getting to your loved
one so it can make their
heart feel whole.

BIOLOGY
101
B = Brown eye
BB x Bb
B
B   BB
B   BB

Now there are stories of
some kisses getting lost or
led astray.
But sheer grit &
determination helped them
always find their way.

There's a drive inside a kiss that keeps them chugging right along when it's an uphill battle and they need to remain strong.

# A kiss will climb the highest mountains

LOVE

and sail the raging seas.

It will clash with the
fiercest storms and will
cross the desert's heat.

Of course, it could encounter issues with some traffic or a crowd. And it may get into trouble going someplace it's not allowed.

5
DANGER
DO NOT
ENTER
HIGH VOLTAGE

They may get caught
up in a thistle

or stuck in a spider's net.

They could get
captured by a blue bird

or distracted by a pet.

PET STORE
OPEN

Sometimes, they can be found clinging to statues in the park

LOVE
PARKING
ROBERT
INDIANA

and can get caught up
helping others and be
out way after dark.

But even if the one
you love is miles and
miles away,
one thing to remember
is that your kiss is on
its way.

It's gearing up to give
that special person
you adore
all the love you
packed inside that
kiss, and even more.

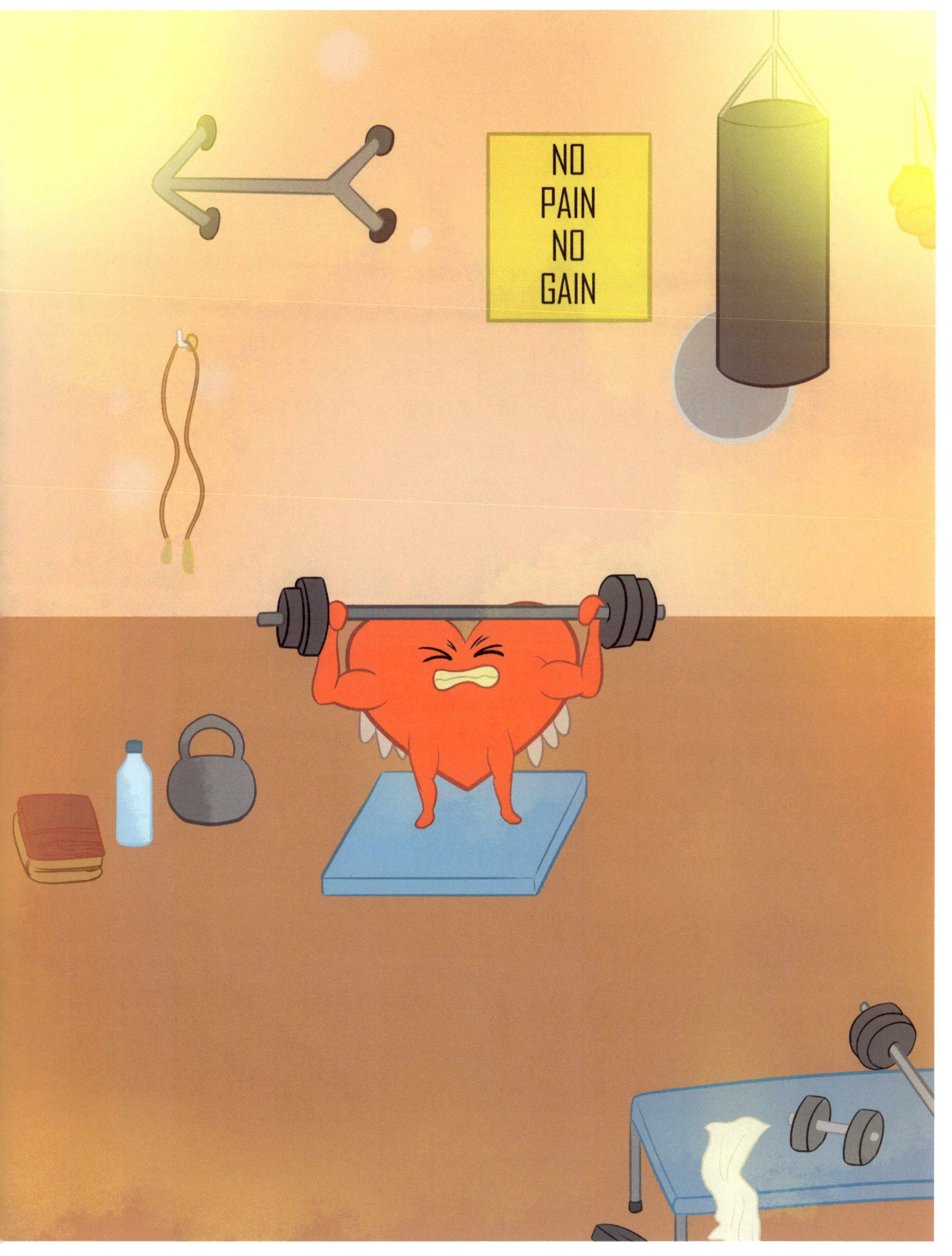
NO
PAIN
NO
GAIN

And just when you start to lose some hope and worry that's the end, another kiss comes 'round the corner and smacks YOU in the head!

It fills you up with love
and warmth and
happiness inside,
and YOU too are left
feeling LOVE from the
one who said "Goodbye".

So, the moral of the
story is when you need
to send a kiss,
to that very special
person that you're surely
going to miss

remember that this little piece of love is meant to share, and never give up hope; a kiss will always make it there.

# THE END

# TIPS FOR DEALING WITH SEPARATION

Simply Blow a Kiss is a story about having to say goodbye to someone you love. For some children, separating from caregivers can be a real struggle. Below are some tips for parents dealing with children experiencing separation anxiety or who may have a hard time separating from caregivers.

1.      Be consistent – Establish a goodbye routine that is simple and stick with it. Whether a special goodbye hug or a comforting phrase, choose something simple you can incorporate daily into your routine that your child will recognize as part of the goodbye process.  Use the same routine each day so your child is comfortable predicting what will come next.

2.      Be patient and positive – Accept that change will not happen overnight and recognize even the smallest wins.  Use positive language and share how proud you are of their efforts and successes no matter how small.

3.          Practice – Talk about the goodbye routine at home or in another comfortable location where your child feels safe.  Ask your child questions about the routine like, What do we do after we hang up your jacket? Or What do I always say after you say I Love You? Use toys or dolls to practice the goodbye routine at home and make sure to end it with a happy reunion.

4.      Establish trust and validate feelings – Follow through on any promises made during goodbyes to establish trust. Be sure to let your child know their feelings are normal and that you also feel badly having to leave them.

5.      Blow a Kiss – Tell your child that you will blow them kisses throughout the day  and remind them that a kiss always makes it.  Ask them to blow you kisses when they feel sad or miss you.  You can talk about how many kisses were blown each day and how you felt each one when a loving thought suddenly popped into your mind.

 *If your child's separation anxiety is severe and is affecting their health or well-being, consider contacting a mental health professional for additional support and strategies.

**Loss**

**A few of the illustrations portray the loss of a loved one.  To send love to someone you have lost simply picture them in your mind and blow them a kiss.  You can do it any place, at any time and this author truly believes that kiss will make it there.  Anytime you send love out into the universe that positive energy is making a difference.**